For Joanie

N.D.

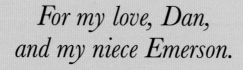

For my love, Dan,
and my niece Emerson.

K.P.

Published by Peter Pauper Press, Inc.
202 Mamaroneck Avenue
White Plains, New York 10601 USA

Published in the United Kingdom and Europe by Peter Pauper Press, Inc.
c/o White Pebble International
Unit 2, Plot 11 Terminus Rd.
Chichester, West Sussex PO19 8TX, UK

Library of Congress Cataloging-in-Publication Data

Names: Dyer, Nick, 1982- author. | Pousette, Kelly, illustrator.
Title: Little things / by Nick Dyer ; illustrated by Kelly Pousette.
Description: First edition. | White Plains, New York : Peter Pauper Press,
Inc., 2019. | Summary: A child admires everyday small things, from
footprints to raindrops to a turtle in need of being flipped upright, that
are small in size but big in beauty and importance.
Identifiers: LCCN 2018046363 | ISBN 9781441328595 (hardcover : alk. paper)
Subjects: | CYAC: Size--Fiction. | Mindfulness (Psychology)--Fiction.
Classification: LCC PZ7.1.D944 Li 2019 | DDC [E]--dc23 LC record available at https://lccn.loc.gov/2018046363

ISBN 978-1-4413-2859-5
Manufactured for Peter Pauper Press, Inc.
Printed in Hong Kong

7 6 5 4 3 2 1

Visit us at www.peterpauper.com

Little Things

By Nick Dyer

Illustrated by Kelly Pousette

PETER PAUPER PRESS, INC.
White Plains, New York

My favorite things…

are little things.

I find them in my pockets,
my shoes,

and in my cereal bowl.

They can be in between
blades of grass,

in the air,

or a million miles away.

I love to hold them,

count them,

and follow them home.

Little things can be yummy things.

They can also become…

...humongous things.

They can show me hidden things,

like very special things.

Little things can seem like big things.

Big things can seem like little things.

And sometimes
little things,

It's easy to
miss the little
things.

So I make sure to
stop and look.

I look under water,

under rocks,

and under other
little things.

And when I do,
little things can
tell me where
I've been,

where I'm going,

what's nearby,

and what's on its way.

Little things are everywhere,

but they're never just
little things.

Because even the littlest thing,

can be a big thing…

...to a little thing.